1

GHOSTS

of the

ILLINOIS

CANAL SYSTEM

© David Youngquist 2008

Dedicated to my lovely wife, Fay.

The reader should understand that we were able to obtain some of these stories only if we promised to obscure the actual identity of persons and/or property. This required us to occasionally use fictitious names. In such cases, the names of the people and/or the places are not to be confused with actual places or actual persons living or dead.

About the Author

D.M. Youngquist has been writing since he could pick up a crayon and make marks on paper. His first work was as an occasional contributor to his High School Newspaper and the local weekly. His first paid work came while attending Western Illinois University. He started as an opinions writer and by the time he graduated with a B.A. in History Education in 1996, he had written for every department of the Western Courier.

After college he briefly worked for a local newspaper as a reporter. His non-fiction work has been published in such magazines as The Carousel Horse News and Trader, American Hunter, and SHOOT! Magazine. One of his short horror stories was published recently by the British webzine DarkfireUK.

This is Youngquist's second book of ghost stories. He currently resides in Tiskilwa, Illinois with his family. He works at the Ace Hardware Retail Support Center in Princeton, IL in order to keep "taters on the table." He is currently shopping around a science fiction novel, while hard at work on a fantasy novel. When not working at the warehouse or on a book, Youngquist enjoys taking his son hunting or his daughter fishing, or hiking with his wife and kids.

Paula Guttilla: Amateur Photographer

My passion for photography started when I received my first camera at the age of 10, a Kodak Brownie. The wonderful photos in the Life Magazines that came weekly to my home also inspired me. Now, whenever I have a break in my busy life, I am either reading, studying, collecting or playing with photography. I was born and raised in Newton, Massachusetts and attended the University of Denver in Colorado. I met my husband, Tom, backpacking in Europe in 1972. I have worked for Jay Baxter CPA for 21 years as an accountant and an enrolled agent. I reside in Utica, IL. and have two grown children.

Preface

It was transportation systems in the 1930's and 1940's that spelled the end of the commercial usefulness of the Illinois Canal System. River traffic was just then coming into its own. An improved highway system was being quickly built. These conspired, with an improved rail system, to muscle the canal system aside and to make it all but irrelevant.

And, it is a transportation system today, our highways, which enable us to speed by that lazy and outdated canal. Except for a few signs and a few crossings, the canal offers little more evidence of its existence today than if it were simply a few more corn rows that could have replaced it. It's easy to forget or ignore the canal. After all, the attractions of modern life tend to take us elsewhere.

But, the canal hasn't forgotten us. There are ghosts along this beautiful stretch of history that are more than willing to remind us of earlier times, earlier loves, and earlier conflicts. There are places along the canal you don't want to go unless you are prepared to be jolted out of your complacency about the canal. There are things you don't want to do unless you are prepared to pay the consequences.

This book tells of the ghosts who yet inhabit the waters and the shores of our beautiful Illinois Canal System. It reminds us there are those who yet inhabit the canal, those who we thought had left us decades ago.

Table of Contents

Introduction

If you ask most people if they believe in ghosts, they look at you as if you're a little eccentric. At least here in the Midwest. Too much in the way of solid German and Swede bloodstock. Get under the surface a little, and it becomes: "Well, I don't believe in ghosts, but this one time...."

This is my second book on ghosts. Many of these stories have not been heard outside of family members or close friends. Others have gotten to be well known in the community. When I talk to folks about this subject, they ask me if I believe in ghosts. I do. I have had too many personal experiences with them not to Some of these first hand experiences are here in this book some are in my last one.

I hope you enjoy this little tome. Remember, the next time your car keys disappear, and you find them hanging in their place six months later, you might not be as forgetful as you thought.

On the Bridge

Princeton, Illinois, is well centered in the state. It's the halfway point between the Quad Cities and Chicago on Interstate 80. As such, it is far enough away from both not to be influenced much by either. Most of the commerce Princeton enjoys comes from that asphalt artery.

Long before highways existed, however, waterways were one method that money came to town. The Hennepin Canal is only three miles to the south, and when the canal was in operation, it was tied to the town not only by employment, but by trade as well.

Barges would dock in Tiskilwa on their trip through the canal. People came from the surrounding area to sell and load their cargo onto the barges. Princeton was only a short drive away.

In the fall of 1930, Mark Johanson set off from Princeton to the Tiskilwa valley to sell a load of corn at the mill. From there, it would be loaded on barges in the canal and shipped to the larger waterways.

The road wound south for four miles then crossed the canal by a steel-girder bridge. Mark eased his truck into a lower gear to make the climb onto the deck of the bridge. With the throttle wide open, he drove up the man-made hill to the bridge. With a bump, he was on the deck.

The strain overheated the truck, however, and with a hiss, the radiator erupted. Steam blew from the top of the brass frame as water boiled away. Mark shut the engine down. It was early morning, and there was little traffic on the road. He could hear a barge in Tiskilwa, but other than that, there was no one around. His truck on the bridge would not be a hindrance to anyone.

In the bed of the truck, Mark found a bucket. He climbed off the bridge, crossed the towpath and made his way to the canal. He sloshed water into the bucket, careful not to drag any moss in. Canal water wasn't the best to dump into the radiator, but it would do, and he could drain it and refill it from the well at home.

Mark scrambled up the near-vertical bank and made his way back to the bridge. As he climbed onto the bridge, another farmer stood in front of his truck.

"Mornin' to you," Mark called.

The man turned. "Mornin'," he nodded.

"Truck boiled over," Mark said. There was a puddle of water under the front end. "I'll have her out of the way shortly."

The man grunted as Mark pulled the cap off the radiator. He slowly poured water in. It bubbled for a brief second then calmed down as he poured the rest in.

"You from here 'bouts?" Mark asked. He knew many of the local farmers but not this gentleman.

"Over ta Indian Valley" the man replied. "This's one of them new automobiles, ain't it?"

Mark considered it for a moment. They hadn't called Tiskilwa "Indian Valley" for better than twenty years. The guy didn't look that old, maybe in his thirties. His clothes were out of date. He hadn't seen anything like those canvas pants and hob-nail boots since he was a little kid and his grandpa wore them around the farm. Maybe the guy was eccentric.

"Well, the truck really isn't new, but it does the job."

"Looks like it pulls more than my team." The man jerked his thumb back over his shoulder. A team of golden Belgian draft horses stood hitched to a large wagon.

Mark wondered how he hadn't heard them as they trotted up the gravel road. "Well, it can pull a lot more, but it's not as good in the field as your team. That's why I've got a tractor at home."

"Can I help?" the man asked.

"Well, you can crank it if you want, and I'll be on my way."

Mark showed the man how to turn the crank on the front of the truck. He warned him not to let the handle kick back, or he'd get a busted arm. Mark climbed into the cab and opened the throttle a hair.

The man cranked. It popped a couple of times, then caught. The engine hummed to life as it pumped the fresh water through its system. Up front, the man stood from his task and grinned at Mark. With a wave, he disappeared.

Mark's jaw gaped open. He looked around the bridge, set the brake and jumped out. The man was gone. He had simply vanished, there was no other way off the bridge. Behind him on the road, the team and their wagon were gone.

Mark climbed back into the cab. His hands shook as he eased the throttle open and put the truck in gear. This was something that he'd have to talk to his wife about when he got home. It was more than he could explain.

Mule Skinner

Jim Stolz shrugged into the harness of his backpack. He had left Milan, Illinois, three days ago to hike the Hennepin Canal. His wife would pick him up in Hennepin, Illinois, in three days. Half the state was a good distance to cover in a week.

Jim had the time in at his job to take a few weeks off every year. At 40, he was still fit enough to use one of those weeks on a backpacking trip. Last year he had hiked the River Trail along the Mississippi, from Moline, Illinois, to Dubuque, Iowa. This year he wanted something different.

Illinois is such a big state. Hundreds of miles long, and two hundred wide, it made for some good hikes. The old canal system provided a nice way to see the state, and, since the Hennepin fell into the Mississippi just a couple of miles from his home in Moline, it was an easy decision to make the trip.

He liked winter hikes. You had the trail to yourself for the most part. Locals would be on the trail around towns, but no long-distance hikers, and he had the campgrounds to himself. The scenery was different, too, in the winter.

A lot of people didn't like the season, as it looked so bare and dead. Jim liked it because you saw things that weren't there in the summer: Bald Eagles drifted above him as they hunted for fish in the canal and the feeder creeks; Deer foraged for acorns among the oaks that grew along the borders, and Canada Geese drifted through the water or fed in the cornfields nearby.

Jim closed in on Wyanet, which was a little past the half-way point of his hike. The crisp air pumped through his lungs as pea gravel crunched under his feet. He passed through the larger campgrounds along the trail. At the lock system outside of Wyanet, he paused to read one of the placards that described the lift bridge and how it operated.

A hundred yards further on, the lockmaster's house stood sentry over the canal. The old white building was boarded up with iron grating secured all of the openings. Two crumbling chimneys sprouted from the roof high above his head.

What had been a yard now contained the fire pits and grills of a state campground. Jim dropped his backpack and set up his tent. On the lone table, he placed his single-burner camp stove. Tomorrow he would stop in Tiskilwa and pick up some fresh food. Maybe have a meal. For now, the dehydrated food he had packed would do.

His supper was prepared to the music of water as it roared over the spillway of the lock. A covey of bobwhite quail called to one another in the field across the canal. Half a mile north, an occasional car passed on Highway 6. Jim read for a bit after supper, then crawled into his sleeping bag for the night.

He woke up slowly, not sure why. His watch read 4:30am. Jim lay there for a moment as trying to go back to sleep. Then he heard it: Chains clanked as hooves clopped through the gravel.

"Git up, Sam, dammit!" A voice drifted to him over the rush of water. "Move on, Bob."

A whip cracked in the morning air. The pace of the hooves picked up briefly, then fell back into their slow rhythm. Chains clanked louder as the sound closed in on his camp. Jim grabbed a flashlight and unzipped the tent. He didn't know anyone around who still worked with teams, except the Amish, and Amish didn't swear.

Jim poked his head out the tent flap and shined the beam of light across the grounds. Nothing. He could hear the chains rattle, and the hooves beat time in the gravel, but he couldn't see anything. He swung the light across the canal. The beam flashed across a small bank of mist.

He didn't think anything of it at first, but when he brought the beam back to the mist he saw movement and thought, "Wait a minute."

As he watched, the mist swirled and crept along the ground. The sound seemed to come from the grey cloud as it moved upstream along the canal. Shouts and swearing came again, followed by the snap of the whip. The mist picked up speed as it moved out of the reach of his flashlight. Jim watched as the fog drew even with the lift-bridge, then dissipated. Only the roar of the spillway was left to fill the night air.

Jim closed his tent, and laid back to stare at the ceiling until dawn lit the nylon. He rolled out, struck camp and shrugged into his backpack without breakfast. At the next lock, he crossed the canal at a small footbridge and continued on down the trail.

A mile further on, he came across the remnants of an old barn. Concrete walls and pillars reached skyward. Glass lay in splinters from windows that had been busted out years before. The wooden structure was rotted away. Inside was open space, with a few pieces of rusted equipment. Jim poked around inside as he snapped a few pictures.

"They sure did love concrete, didn't they?" A voice shattered the morning. Jim jumped and spun on his heel.

"Sorry, didn't mean to scare you like that." A man in his mid-thirties smiled at him. His dog sat beside him on the trail.

"Just didn't hear you come up is all," Jim said as his heart bounced around his ribcage.

"I like to take my dog out before I go to work. This's a nice stretch. We can get a couple miles in."

"What was this place?" Jim asked as he ran his hand over one of the smooth walls.

"Well, they used a lot of mules and horses to dig this canal. This was one of the barns they kept 'em in. They were staged up and down the canal. I think this is about the last barn left."

Jim felt his knees go weak as he leaned into the wall.

"You okay, Mister?" the younger man asked.

"Yeah, just didn't sleep well is all. Tired."

With a wave and a call to his dog, the man left. Jim picked up his pack and swung it onto his shoulders. Next trip he'd camp further along.

Court is Always in Session

Hennepin, Illinois, grew up at a bend of the Illinois River. It was a good place for barges to put in to take on cargo. It was the first landing that could be reached from the Illinois and Michigan Canal while it was in operation. It grew even more when the Hennepin Canal opened slightly upstream from there.

The city became an important commercial hub in central Illinois. As such, it became the county seat of Putnam County. A large red brick courthouse was erected two blocks from the river. Hennepin spread into the cornfields and timber from there. Roads that followed the river came to an end in town.

Then the canals closed. The I and M closed first since it was too narrow for modern barges. Railroads had taken the place of most of the interstate shipping. Then in 1956, the Hennepin Canal closed. It had never been a profitable venture, and by that time, trucking had combined with the railroads to put the final nail in the coffin of cross-state barges.

For more than a decade, both the population and businesses of Hennepin dwindled. By the late 1960s the town was nearly nonexistent. A number of homes and businesses on the edge of town were boarded up, and the property returned to cornfields.

Then ground was broken for a new steel mill. A huge operation, it employed hundreds of people to build it, and hundreds more to operate the plant once it was open.

In 1970, Chris Hopper moved to town with his young wife, Shelly. They were from Peoria, but small town life appealed to them, and Chris's uncle got him a job at the mill as a crane operator. They bought an old home on the west side of the town square and began their family.

Shelly would often take walks around town. Both for exercise and to get to know her neighbors. Her walks would often take her past the courthouse, which was just across the park from her home. There were times she would feel uneasy as she strolled past the old brick building. Times when she felt she was being watched, even when court was closed for business.

One spring morning, the baby kicked her awake. She was seven months along and quite ready to be done being pregnant. Chris was at the mill and wouldn't be home for a couple of hours, so rather than lay there and be uncomfortable, she decided to go for a walk.

Shelly stepped out of the house and drew the clean morning air into her lungs. Dew was heavy on the grass and glittered in the fading moonlight. She set off around the park.

As she neared the courthouse, the uneasy feeling washed

over her again. Something didn't feel right. She felt as if she were in a huge crowd. As if there were people on all sides of her. Out of instinct she pushed against them, then realized that no one was there.

Shelly glanced up at the large entrance of the courthouse and screamed. Two bodies hung in midair. The necks of the corpses were wrenched to the side as they spun on an invisible tether. The bodies slowly turned, and she could hear the creak of rope that held a heavy weight.

Finally the bodies faced her, illuminated by the moonlight. Both dead men stared at her, faces frozen in surprise and pain. Shelly took a step backwards, hand to her mouth. The dead eyes held hers. For long seconds she stood there. Then a man blinked.

Shelly's breath caught in her throat as the man blinked again, then a long, greasy smile crossed his face. She screamed and didn't care who heard her. She screamed her throat raw as both men grinned down at her, and disappeared.

Running as hard as she could across the park back to her house, she slammed the door and threw the lock. The baby tumbled around inside her as she gasped for breath.

For long minutes, she stood there, her back to the door. Finally Shelly convinced herself that it couldn't be real. Men couldn't hang there in midair. Slowly she lifted the curtain of the kitchen window and peeked over at the courthouse.

The moon and the streetlights cast enough light on the courthouse steps that Shelly could see everything: The columns, the doors with their heavy bronze handles, the handrails. Everything was as is should be. And no bodies.

After that morning, Shelly always walked as far away from the courthouse as possible, if she went out alone. Before the baby was born, she did a little investigating. She discovered that in the 1800's-when the courthouse was built- criminals sentenced to death were hanged at the entrance to the building. The ropes ran through the ceiling and back into the attic of the building to securely anchor them to internal beams.

In 1854, Thomas Johnson and William Moore were hanged there in Hennepin for River Piracy on the Illinois River. Shelly became one of the people convinced that they never completely left the courthouse.

Wedding March

Buda, Illinois, sprouts off either side of Illinois State Route 40. Trains run through the tiny town that sits on a knob of ground in the middle of the Illinois prairie. On the main drag is a bait-and-tackle shop. Fishing is an important part of life in Buda. There are two state parks nearby that produce excellent fishing. One is the site of old strip mines, the other is the Hennepin Canal.

Barges used to dock north of Buda, when the canal was in operation. Rivermen would come to come town by trolley line and find a meal or a room for the night. One of the first buildings they passed as they came into town was the old Methodist church.

By the mid 1980s, however, the church was at the end of its useful life. The small congregation had not been able to keep up the maintenance, and eventually, it was more cost effective to build a new structure rather than repair the old.

On the appointed day, people gathered one last time in the building, then locked the doors behind them. For a decade the old church sat vacant. No longer useful as a house of God yet still Methodist property, it was, therefore, a liability. When Terry Grimes approached Pastor John Criton with an offer to by the building, the diocese found an agreeable way to part with it.

"Mom, I really don't want to move clear up there," Jessie Grimes said. She packed her clothes into a cardboard box and taped it shut. "I don't know anyone up there."

"That's why we're moving in June," Caroline said, "This way you've got a few weeks to meet new people and get used to the area before school starts."

"It's in the middle of nowhere." Jesse whined.

"It's a great school system, with a brand-new high school," Caroline said. She gathered a box of clothes and headed for the door. "Besides, after that kid was caught with a gun in his locker this spring, I don't feel safe with you at school here anymore."

Jessie rolled her eyes as she followed her mom to the truck. "I'm glad I've got my license, at least I can go somewhere."

Her mother sighed in response. It had taken two years to convert the church into a home. The place was beautiful; they even retained the stained-glass windows, but it would be an adjustment for all of them.

That summer was spent putting the house in final order. The yard was replanted, flower beds were cleaned and a garage was added to the structure. It became quite a nice home.

Through the summer, Jessie worked in the town of Princeton, not far down the highway. She met new people and made friends with several girls who also went to Bureau Valley High School. She did keep in touch with her friends in Peoria, but sixty miles is a long distance between people.

Jessie spent a lot of time with Haylee, who was in the same class she was at the high school. Haylee thought it was neat that her friend lived in an old church. The sanctuary was converted into a living room, complete with high, vaulted ceilings.

"I still don't like the place," Jessie said. The two girls stretched out on her bed as they listened to a disc in the stereo.

"What's not to like? It's beautiful," Haylee said.

"It's not what it looks like," Jessie said. "I don't know. Sometimes it's just creepy."

"How can a church be creepy?"

"I don't know," Jessie paused. "Just don't tell anyone I said this, but sometimes I hear voices out there."

"Voices?"

"Yeah, but real low like. I can't understand what they're saying. It's more like people talking in church-real quietly."

"Okay, I'll take your word for it. Sure it's not a radio or something?" Haylee asked.

"Pretty sure," Jessie said.

With a shrug, the topic turned to other things.

The week before school started, the girls decided that a sleepover at Jesse's house, followed by a day of shopping in Peoria, was called for. It was an uneventful night of movies and popcorn. They talked on the instant message boards with their friends and finally fell asleep a little after midnight.

At six o'clock the next morning, Jessie's eyes popped open.

"Haylee, hear that?" she hissed.

"Hear what?" Haylee mumbled into her pillow.

"Listen. Voices."

Haylee rolled over, still half asleep. Sure enough, she could hear the voices this time, too. Quietly, the girls slid out of bed and tip-toed down the hall. The voices grew louder, but they still couldn't understand what was being said.

They got to the end of the hall, crouched down, and peeked around the corner into the living room. Jessie drew a breath to scream, but Haylee clamped her hand over her friend's mouth.

At the front of the room, about two feet above the floor, stood a bride and groom. He wore a black tux, complete with tails, and she donned a white gown that flowed down the three steps that used to reach the altar. They peered into one another's eyes as they repeated garbled vows, then turned and faced the invisible audience.

The girls watched as the couple, beaming with an unearthly light, descended the missing stairs to the floor of the living room. As they walked up what had been the main aisle of the sanctuary, the couple first passed through the coffee table, then the couch before they walked into the hall. At the door, they disappeared.

"Well, now we know where the voices came from," Haylee said. "Now what?"

"Now I think we have Mom make us some coffee, and we get out of here for the day." Jessie stood on shaky legs. "I wonder why they're still here?"

"Don't know," Haylee said. "It's not like you hear of a haunted church every day."

Hangman's Tree

The Illinois and Michigan Canal was built in the early 1800s, at the height of the canal-building era in the United States. It connected Lake Michigan in the east to the Illinois River in the west, through its waterways it connected Chicago to the world. Towns grew up around the I and M Canal, most notably Chicago, but the canal gave life to other towns as well.

The old canal ends its journey in LaSalle, which, along with its sister city Peru, is a thriving community now fed as much by Interstate 80 as it is by the Illinois River. The I and M saw its last barge lock out in the early 1930s, and is now a recreational destination for thousands of people each year.

As with every town, where there is life, there is death. Some of the older cemeteries in LaSalle went out of use after 100 years and have become forgotten. Others continue to grow and take in new residents for their eternal sleep.

One such old burial site is Riverview Cemetery on the eastern side of the Illinois River. The last person was interred there in the 1950s, two decades after the I and M closed down. The cemetery is well maintained, however, and has a staff that takes care of the grounds.

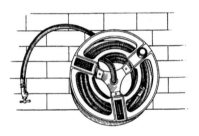

Unfortunately, it has also become a hot-spot for ghost hunters. Local legend has it that Satanists once used the grounds for their unholy rites. They disturbed the spirits of those buried there and the dead are now restless in their sleep.

Bob Hopper lived and worked in LaSalle most of his life. His children lived with their mother however, in Kentucky. It made for a rough relationship with his kids to have them so far away. This year he had the kids for the holidays-the first time in the seven years since his divorce. He showed the kids around town and entertained them as single parents are wont to do.

The kids renewed friendships from their early school years. Caitlyn had only moved to Kentucky only two years earlier, so was in contact with her friends on a regular basis.

"It's true," Mandy said as she stuffed French fries into her mouth. "The old cemetery is haunted."

"Mandy, there is no such thing as ghosts," Caitlyn said. She took a pull of her soda. "People just use those stories the scare each other. They've been doing it since the dawn of time." She was sixteen that year, and therefore knew everything.

"All I'm saying, Cait, is that I've seen some pretty hairy stuff down there at night."

"All in your imagination, Mandy. I'll go down there with you tonight and we'll prove it one way or another."

That afternoon, Caitlyn asked to be able to go out with Mandy that night. When Bob asked what they were going to do, Caitlyn told him the truth. She didn't want to lie to her dad and possibly not be welcome back for a visit. Besides, as the sun went down, the thought got a little more spooky.

It was a cold night as Bob pulled the car off the street on the back side of Riverview Cemetery. He didn't like ghosts or ghost stories or even the thought of being in a graveyard after dark. They were bad enough during the day. Still, he would rather know his daughter and her friends were safe than have some manmade evil happen to them.

Inside the cemetery grounds, small lights bounced off the tombstones and the trees. They swirled around to rest in places, then moved on. Dark shadows were outlined by the glow. Then one of the lights shined on Bob and Caitlyn.

"'Bout time you showed up," Mandy's voice whispered out of the dark. "I didn't think you'd make it. That your Dad?"

The light flashed into Bob's eyes. He held up his hand to shadow them from the sudden brightness. "It's me, Mandy. Who're the rest of these folks?"

"Hi, Mister Hopper. These are some friends of mine. They're amateur ghost hunters." She moved the beam of the flashlight back to the ground. "We've been wanting to come out here for a while now. Caity just gave us an excuse."

"Great," Bob muttered. He pulled a flashlight of his own from his car, handed another to Caitlyn, and they set off.

For an hour they methodically crisscrossed the grounds. On occasion someone would get an unusual reading from a meter and make note. Digital cameras lit the stones with their flashs. Bob's uneasiness grew as they worked their way further in.

"I've got to take a leak," Bob said.

"Daddy!"

"Sorry. Tea doesn't keep long when it's cold." Bob grinned. "I'll be right back."

Bob walked a few feet away after a soft warning to keep the flashlights pointed in a safe direction. His own light was clamped in his teeth as he stepped under a tree that overlooked the river. He stood there for a few seconds and watched a barge make the swing around a bend. The flashlight dropped from his mouth.

"Damn," he whispered. Bob reached out to lean against the tree. A jolt hit him as he touched the bark. So many sensations washed over him. Fear was mingled with hate. Sorrow and terror pulsed through him. He started to cry for no reason, but the tears were heavy on his lashes.

Like a hammer blow, a sharp pain slammed into his neck. A strobe of white light flared behind his eyes. With a gasp, he sank to his knees beside the ancient oak.

"You okay, Daddy?" Caitlyn asked as she ran up.

"I've got to go," Bob croaked.

"Daddy, what's wrong?" She placed her hand on his shoulder as he began to stand.

Bob picked up his flashlight. "I don't feel good. I'll meet you at the car."

"You're not leaving by yourself," Caitlyn said. She put an arm around her father's shoulder, and together they left the grounds.

Bob slid into the driver's seat of the car and took a few deep breaths. "Sorry I ruined your night, honey. You go, back if you want."

"That's okay, Daddy. I was starting to get creeped out anyway. Let's just go home."

Bob drove back to the house. The rest of the visit was filled with family events and distractions, but his reaction that night to the old tree was frequently in the back of his mind.

A few weeks later, after the kids were back with their mom, Bob swung by the old cemetery again. In the daylight it wasn't such a bad place. Quiet. Peaceful. A groundskeeper was there, cleaning up the winter debris. Bob struck up a conversation with the old man and finally asked him about the old tree in the back. The one that overlooked the river.

The old man told him that the old tree had been used as a gallows many times. Sometime by vigilantes, sometimes by the law. A lot of murderers, thieves and river pirates had swung from those branches. The old man spat a wad of tobacco juice into the leaves.

"So why don't you folks cut it down?" Bob asked.

The old man grinned sideways at him. " 'Cause ever time my guys gets near the damned thing, they get sick."

Split Rock

The ice ages that flattened most of Illinois left behind more than fertile soil in their retreat. Many rocks of all sizes and shapes remained from the grinding sheets of ice. For years they clattered against plows, were dug up in the construction of roads or were grazed around by livestock. They range in size from pebbles to pickup trucks.

On occasion, erosion from the melted glacier does the work to expose slabs of rock not found other places. These monsters have to be dealt with for human endeavors to move forward.

One such vein of rock, in this case something known as Saint Peter's Sandstone, was exposed between the towns of Utica and LaSalle. How far into the earth it descends is a mystery. All anyone knows is that it was there long before white men set foot in the Illinois River Valley.

When the builders of the Illinois and Michigan Canal came to the sandstone cliff, they assumed the canal could be rerouted. They assumed wrong. It was far too massive. The farm ground was too soft to support a canal bed, so the engineers decided the next best thing would be to go through the rock and continue on the original path.

Months of drilling and blasting carved a notch through the sandstone. A tunnel was also drilled through the south side of the rock, in order to allow cranes and equipment to be brought into the canal bed more easily. Split Rock is a landmark today, and the tunnel is open to anyone brave enough to crawl into it.

Jim Hanson was one such person. He and his girlfriend were on a fishing trip with his buddy, Ray Watts. The couples met several times a week to socialize. This Saturday, they planned to spend the day together before they grilled the catch.

They parked in Utica and hiked down the canal. It was a nice spring day, with the leaves just starting to bud on the trees.

The girls were along to make their men happy. They had both fished with their daddies as little girls but hadn't been since fish started to smell and shopping got interesting. But to prove they weren't just a couple of city girls, Jill and Tammy agreed to go with on this trip. Three of the group had been to Split Rock a number of times. Jim, being an import from Bettendorf, Iowa, wasn't familiar with the area.

Ahead of them, the rock reared up out of the ground like a silent sentinel.

"Cool," Jim said. "I wonder if you can climb up on it."

"Sandstone," Tammy said as she took her hand out of his. She shifted her gear and dropped it on the trail. "It's crumbly and slick. Seems like every year someone breaks his neck trying to climb it."

They walked around the area for a few minutes. They had seen the rock all their lives, but with Jim there, they could appreciate its novelty even more.

Jim ran his hand across the surface as he gazed up at the top. "Wow," he muttered.

"Yeah," Ray said. "Makes you realize how tough them old Irish boys were. Dig this ditch by hand, then have to blast through this rock? Tougher than me." They set up their poles and wet their lines. Morning was young yet, and the fish were biting after their long winter fast. Soon the basket was brimming with fish they decided to take a break.

"So this is the tunnel, huh?" Jim asked. He ran his hand around the smooth edge at the mouth.

"Yep," Jill said. "Creepy place."

"Oh please!" Jim snorted. "Nothin' in there that shouldn't be. Just bats and other animals."

"Bats are enough to keep me out," Tammy said. She shivered in the warm spring sun.

"Some say it's haunted, too," Ray said. He stood at the entrance, thumbs hooked in the front pockets of his jeans.

"Haunted by what? Skunks?" Jim chuckled.

"Don't know. I've never been in it," Ray said.

"You guys have lived here all your lives, and you've never been in that thing?"

They all nodded.

"Well, I'm going in." Jim said. He rummaged in his tackle box and brought out a flashlight. With a grin and a wink, he stepped into the darkness.

"Jim, get out of there," Tammy said.

"You come in."

"No."

"Chicken."

With a frustrated sigh, she stepped into the depths. Ray and Jill followed. The four poked around inside for a few minutes. They found the normal detritus of nearly two hundred years: broken tools, rusted beer cans, cigarette butts. Tucked away in one corner was a pair of panties some girl had lost. Jill and Tammy wondered how anyone could fool around in such a place.

Jim shined his light onto the ceiling. Bats clung to the sandstone and fluttered nervously as the beam touched them. Some scattered from their perches to fly about the tunnel.

"Come on," Tammy said, "let's get out of here now."

"Yeah, okay," Jim said. He swung the beam back the way they had come in. It fell on the form of a man. With a gasp, everyone jumped. They thought they were alone in the tunnel.

"You scared us, Mister," Ray said.

The man didn't move. He stood there staring into the light. He didn't lift a hand. On his head was an old-fashioned derby with a tattered silk band and chunks missing from the brim. He wore a faded flannel shirt and his pants were brown canvas, held up by a pair of thick suspenders.

"You okay, Mister?" Jim asked.

The man didn't move. "Fire in the hole," he whispered.

"What?" Tammy said.

"Fire in the hole," the man said again. He opened his mouth wide and screamed. His voice rose like a fire whistle. One long note that never wavered in pitch. The couples covered their ears in a vain attempt to block the pain. At the height of insanity, the man exploded in a flash of light. They saw his body torn apart by a blast and expected to be hit by pieces, but he simply disappeared.

They looked at one another for a split second. Jill crossed herself.

"Christ on the cross," Jim whispered.

As one, they raced for the mouth of the tunnel. Outside they packed their gear, collected the fish, and ran back down the canal to their car.

"Guess the place is haunted," Jim said as he threw his gear in the back of the truck.

"I think you could say that," Tammy agreed.

"You guys ever seen anything like that before?" Jill asked.

Everyone shook their heads. Together they climbed into the truck and headed home. They would fish the canal again, but they had seen all they wanted to of the tunnel.

Cry Baby Bridge

New Bedford is nothing more than a dot on the Bureau County, Illinois, maps. It sits by itself on the fringe of the Illinois Sand Prairie, with its tiny population. Folks that live there work in other towns, miles away. Shopping is done before they come home for the day, as there are no businesses in town. The grade school was closed years ago. It now houses a small seed processing plant for prairie grasses.

Since the soil of the area is composed mostly of sand, agriculture pursuits are accomplished with the help of irrigation. To the east of town, the Green River flows from the north until it ends its journey. To the west of town runs the feeder branch of the Hennepin Canal itself. When the canal was dug, farmers in the area were afraid that the water for the canal would drain their water tables. So the engineers tapped into the Rock River to the north to keep the canal flowing. Still, with all these waterways, there is little in New Bedford to do.

"I'm tellin' you, it's true," Debbie Krantz took a drag of the cigarette she'd lifted from her mom's purse. She flicked the ash on the ground.

"Ain't no way it's real," Carrie said. She waved the smoke away from her face as her friend exhaled. "Dead's dead. No such thing as ghosts."

The two dangled their feet off the tailgate of Debbie's Ranger pickup. They didn't have enough money between them to do much. It was twenty miles either way to Princeton or Sterling. By the time they bought gas, they wouldn't have enough for a cheeseburger apiece, so they were stuck for the day.

"Well, seems to me there's only one way to prove it," Debbie said. "We take the truck out there tonight and try it."

"Fine," Carrie said. She waved away another cloud of smoke.

For the next few hours, they chatted online with their friends. They told some of their plans, and a few wanted to come. Before long three more girls were up for the trip. Many of their friends had heard the legend, and didn't want to press the issue themselves, but they did want a full report.

Round about midnight, Debbie and Carrie slipped out of the house. They had the supplies they needed, along with their cell phones to text their friends. To the east of town, they met the other three at a little gravel road. The other girls hopped into the bed of the small pickup.

Debbie drove onto the middle of the bridge and stopped. She hopped out with Carrie and walked around to the hood. There she sprinkled a light skiff of baby powder. She repeated the process on the rear bumper.

"Okay, now what?" Carrie asked.

"Now we wait." Debbie said as she pulled the handle to take off the emergency brake. The truck idled in neutral as they waited. The girls were silent. Normally, a chatty group, it just wasn't a night to carry on a conversation.

Carrie's 'phone chirped. She jumped and reached for the little thing. One of her friends wanted an update. She texted back that nothing had happened. For another five minutes they sat there. Along the river, a Great Horned Owl called out to the night.

"This's nuts," Carrie said. "How long we supposed to sit here?"

"I don't know," Debbie said. "Maybe...."
The engine sputtered for a half beat, and the headlights dimmed. Then the truck started to roll backward. Slowly at first, it gained speed. Debbie whipped her head around and steered in a straight line. One of the girls in the truck bed started to scream, but another clamped her hand over the screamer's mouth.

In just seconds, they were off the bridge. Debbie turned the wheel and coasted onto the gravel road they had parked at earlier.

She set the brake again and hopped out. Carrie ran around the other side. Her breath came in gulps. Debbie shined a flashlight on the hood as the others gathered around. There in the powder were two sets of tiny handprints.

"Well?" Debbie asked.

"Okay, you proved it," Carrie said. "I-I, still don't know what to think about it."

"I gotta pee," one of the girls said. "Take me home." Carrie aimed the camera in her phone at the prints and snapped a picture. The image was texted around to friends along with the message of what happened.

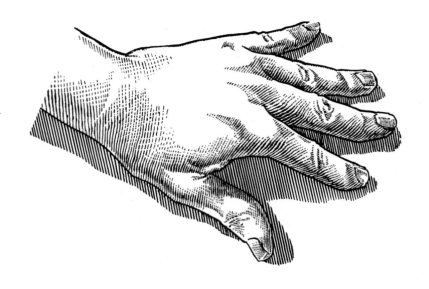

Down by the Rock

The village of Utica is a beautiful little spot on the Illinois River. Tourists come during much of the year to visit Starved Rock State Park and other state parks in the area. Shops in town carry high quality souvenirs to remember the trip. An Irish pub on the main street serves ice cold beer and filling meals for a decent price.

Utica is one of the towns that the Illinois and Michigan canal built. Barges stopped in town to load and unload both freight and passengers. Commerce grew the town long before tourism. Today, the stretch between Utica and LaSalle is one of the few that has been restored and carries water. All the work to restore the canal at this point was done by volunteers, and much of the money used was donated.

The Irish flavor of the Utica is a holdover from the days when the I & M was built. Much of the labor force used to dig the trench was Irish, both Catholic and Protestant. While the work got done, much of the animosity between the two groups followed from Eire. Once the canal was finished, however, many of the workers settled in the area to farm and raise families.

Kevin Finley left his house early one morning to take a run down the towpath of the canal. His normal route took him through town and west along the canal toward LaSalle. He wanted something different today, however, and turned east when he got to the canal.

The towpath was overgrown a bit on this route. Still, it was nice to be alone on the trail some mornings. Kevin trotted along through the tall grass. The birds sang in the summer sunshine. The sun raised its head over the eastern horizon, so the crickets still sang. A squirrel bounced across his path on occasion, barking in protest at the invasion of its territory.

As Kevin neared Buffalo Rock, he noticed that things had begun to quiet down. It was subtle, but there were none of the sounds that had surrounded him before. The birds went silent, the bugs ended their songs. Even the wind died off. It struck him as strange, so he slowed his pace.

Something just didn't feel right, as he stopped to catch his breath. Kevin tried to pass it off as nerves, but there was no reason for him to be worried about anything. He heard it then. Shouts drifted through the woods around him. Not just one or two, but hundreds of voices rose in anger.

He set off to find the source of the ruckus. There was no reason for a large group to be down here. It could get crowded with a half dozen people on this part of the trail, let alone as many as he was hearing. Kevin walked up the canal slowly. The voices got louder, but he still couldn't understand what the people said. It didn't sound friendly though, and he wondered if it were some Klan rally.

Kevin could see Buffalo Rock now, high over his head a quarter mile up. The canal began to fill with mist. He could barely see the floor of the passage as he struggled forward. The fog climbed up over the rim, to spill off into the woods. Still the voices shouted as he headed toward the sound. He was almost on them.

"Hey, what's going on?" Kevin called.

He stopped. He had to be right where they were. It was if the voices were all around him, yet he could see only vague forms in the bed of the canal. He pulled his cell phone from his belt as he slid into the dry bed and weeds tangled around his legs.

"What the hell is going on?" Kevin shouted again. "You keep this up, I'm callin' the cops."

He punched 911 into the phone, and was about to hit send when a volley of gunshots ripped the morning air. He dove to the ground, his phone flipped into the weeds.

"Jesus Christ," Kevin whispered. The shots became more random after the first volley. The voices faded away as the crowd dispersed around him. He glanced up as another shot was fired. The muzzle flash burned through the mist. He ducked back into the weeds. He could hear footsteps around him but saw no one.

The fog began to lift as the voices faded away. High above him, he could see Buffalo Rock again. The bed of the canal cleared. The fog dissipated. Kevin fumbled through the marsh grass to find his phone. He snatched it up and dialed 911 frantically. Then he saw the bodies.

In the grass-not twenty feet away-lay three crumpled forms. Kevin stumbled toward them. He leaned over the nearest one and reached out, touching the man's shoulder. The man rolled over and stared at Kevin, mouth agape, with black empty eye sockets. Blood oozed through his worn flannel shirt in several places. His battered bowler hat lay in the weeds beside him.

Kevin leapt back, but the empty eyes still seemed to stare up at him. He ran over to the other men. They were the same: bullet riddled and dead. One man's face had been blown away, while the others' guts lay spilled across the weeds.

Kevin stood back, heaving as his stomach threatened to empty. With his thumb, he hit the send button on his phone. The operator answered and asked for his emergency. Just as he started to say that people had been shot, the wind picked up. It bent the grass over as it blew down the canal to the west. One of the men's shirts fluttered in the wind. A hat bounced away down the canal, and the men vanished.

"Nothing, Ma'am. Nothing at all," Kevin said. "Sorry to bother you."

"Sir, wait," the dispatcher said. "We can help. What is the emergency?"

"Nothing," Kevin said. He clicked the end button.

He ran his hand through the grass where one of the men had lain. There was still a slight depression in the weeds. His hand came away with a red smear across the palm. Then, it too, faded. He stumbled back to his house, shaking all the way.

Kevin did some research the on canal, and found that at one point there was a strike among the Irish labor force. It came to a confrontation near Buffalo Rock, and was ended when the sheriff and his deputies fired into the crowd. Three men died.

Turkey Hollow

Water has always been important to the village of Milan, Illinois. It grew up between the Mississippi and Rock Rivers. Several large creeks flow through town. At one time fifteen grist mills produced flour and corn meal here so the town originally was named Mill Land. Midwest farmers, with their need to shorten all names, eventually changed the name of the village to Milan. The town was the natural setting for the engineers who designed the Hennepin Canal to end their journey.

The Hennepin empties into the Rock River just above town. Barges then followed the flow of the river back into a series of locks that took them through town and into the Mississippi from there. Barge traffic still brings money into Milan, and the rest of the Quad Cities.

The Hennepin Canal now is a recreational destination for people from the Quad Cities and surrounding areas. Modern barges and tugs are too large to navigate the canal but fishing boats, canoes and kayaks can still navigate both rivers and canal.

A county blacktop known as Turkey Hollow Road runs south of Milan. It winds up out of the river valley and into the more rural reaches of Rock Island County. Several gravel section roads peel off of the blacktop to reach further into the farmland.

One of these roads winds its way into the timberland of the county. After several twists, it drops into a deep valley. The bottom of the valley has been cleared away for pasture, and several farmers raise cattle on the steep hillsides. Other folks raise sheep and more than a few of the smaller places have horses.

One such farm was the old Cove place. A vast menagerie of animals filled the barns, from horses and cattle to chickens and sheep. The farm was built in the early 1900s. Most of the barns were original, with a few modern buildings.

The old house, though, was another matter. It was a huge two-story Victorian that sat away from the road. The large oak trees that grew in the yard offered shade in the summer and acted as a windbreak in the winter. By the 1970s, though, the old home was uninhabited.

A house trailer sat beside one of the newer barns. The big home was in too much disrepair and too expensive to heat in the winter, so the Cove family lived in the trailer and used the house for storage. On occasion, it was rented out to family friends who needed a place to stay.

Brian Jones and Chuck Johanson moved into the Cove farm in the summer of 1977. Both had graduated from the same high school the year before and wanted to get out on their own. Both had jobs at the tractor plants in town. Brian worked at Deere on second shift, Chuck at International Harvester on third.

Saturday morning, Brian poured a cup of coffee as he scrambled some eggs he'd gotten from the chicken house. Chuck pulled into the driveway and parked. Brian poured his friend a glass of orange juice. Chuck would sleep now until at least noon. They greeted one another as Chuck fell into a chair at the table.

They talked about their days and life in general as they ate. Girlfriends came and went, vacations were planned. Then the subject turned to other matters.

"Hey, let me ask you a question," Brian said.

"What's that?" Chuck asked around a mouthful of egg.

"I know we're trying to save money on electricity, but do you have to unscrew all the light bulbs when you leave for work?"

Chuck paused for a moment. "Me? I was going to ask you the same thing. They're always unscrewed when I wake up."

Brian took a pull on his coffee. "Well, it ain't me."

"Ain't me either," Chuck said.

"Well, what the hell is it then?"

"Got me. Maybe one of the Coves?"

"Maybe, but I wouldn't know why. I'll ask Hattie later."

After breakfast, Chuck went upstairs. He took a shower, pulled the drapes and crashed into bed. Brian had a few errands to run, then spent much of the morning under the hood of his truck. Hattie Cove came by later in the day to visit, and he asked her about the bulbs. She knew nothing about it and suggested he make sure they were tight before he left the house.

So the boys agreed. Each would check the bulbs before he left the house for his shift. Each would leave a note for the other to say the lights were in order. For a week this worked. Then one day, they were unscrewed again.

The note Brian left said he checked them. Chuck asked when his friend got home, and Brian swore they were tight when he left. It continued from there. On one occasion, at three o'clock in the morning, the TV blared to life. Brian leapt out of bed, flipped on the lights, and got nothing. With a curse, he found the flashlight he kept beside the bed, went downstairs and turned off the knob on the set. He checked, but was alone in the house.

He screwed the bulbs back into their sockets and tried to go back to sleep. A half hour later, Brian was stirred again as the TV snapped on. This time he didn't even bother with the lights. He simply grabbed the flashlight, went downstairs and yanked the cord from the wall.

Chuck found Brian sitting in a chair, red-eyed and rumpled, when he came in from work.

"What the hell is up with you?" Chuck asked.

"TV kept comin' on," Brian mumbled.

"What do you mean, 'the TV kept comin' on?'"

"The knob kept turnin' on. Twice. I yanked the cord second time."

Chuck tried the light switch. He got nothing. "You okay, man?"

"No," Brian said. "We got to move out, man."

"Let's not get crazy. This house is old. The wiring is screwy, that's all."

"Okay. A little longer, but this keeps up, I'm movin' into my folks fishing house down on the lakes."

For a couple more weeks, the boys stayed in the house. They did little more than eat and sleep there however. They spent many hours with their girlfriends or over at friends' homes. At noon one day, Chuck thought he'd heard footsteps in the hall outside his room. He got up to see who it was, only to find he was alone in the house. He lay in bed for an hour, unable to get back to sleep, then went out and slept in the cab of his truck.

One muggy Sunday night in June, a thunderstorm boiled up over the Quad Cities area. It had been building all day, and cut loose around eight in the evening. Lightning slashed through the sky as thunder rolled through the valley. It shook the house to its foundation. Windows rattled in their frames as the wind threatened to blast through the glass.

The boys sat in Chuck's room and listened to music over the storm. Heavy metal poured from the record player as they talked about girls and work. Lightning added strobe to the pounding pulse of the music.

A tree exploded on top of the hill as lightening reached out a finger to destroy it. The house below shook as the lights went out. Inside, the boys cursed.

"I'll get some candles," Chuck said. Lightning flashed again, and he glanced out the window. "Hey, what's that?"

Brian followed his friend's finger as Chuck pointed at the window. Silhouetted against the flash was something with long, upswept horns. Ears drooped from the side of its narrow skull. Broad shoulders nearly filled the frame. It went dark as the lightning died away.

"Oh hell, the cows are out." Brian said as he started to strand up. "We better go tell the Coves." Lightning flashed again, and the form was gone.

"Wait," Chuck said. "It can't be cows. We're on the second floor."

Brian froze. His friend was right. They were on the second story. The cows couldn't be seen in even if they were in the yard. "What the hell was that thing?"

"I don't know, but I'm not stickin' around to find out." Chuck leapt up. He rushed downstairs in his bare feet, grabbed his keys and headed for the door. "You comin'?" he shouted to Brian.

"Right behind you, man."

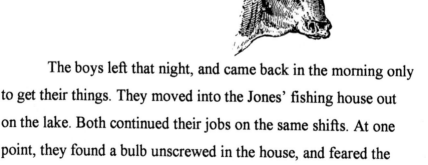

The boys left that night, and came back in the morning only to get their things. They moved into the Jones' fishing house out on the lake. Both continued their jobs on the same shifts. At one point, they found a bulb unscrewed in the house, and feared the thing had followed. It didn't take long to figure out that the semi traffic on the highway fifty yards from the house shook the bulb loose. After that, they simply screwed it in tight.

Later that year, though, both were sitting in a tavern when the subject of old houses came up with the guy who sat next to them. They had never met the man before, but when Chuck mentioned they had lived in the Cove house down in Turkey Hollow earlier in the year, the man paused for a minute.

"Son," he snorted into his beer, "don't you know that's the most haunted house in the county? That's why Hattie and Cliff don't live in it no more."

McLaughlin House

Moline, Illinois, was built by three things: Farming, industry, and river traffic. The open prairie both east and west of the river is fertile ground for crops and livestock. Industry built the tools that the farmers needed, and the river and canals moved crops and industrial product out to the rest of the world. Moline and Rock Island were thriving communities when Chicago was nothing more than a collection of huts on the mud flats of Lake Michigan.

William McLaughlin was one of the more prosperous industrialists of the 1800s. His equipment was shipped all over the world. It made him a rich man. As such, he built a house befitting his status.

His products reached Chicago and eastward from the port in the Quad Cities, traveling through both the Hennepin Canal and the Illinois and Michigan Canal. Barges did cost, but at the height of production, were slightly cheaper than the rail traffic that moved other men's products east.

McLaughlin was a rich man, at least in hard assets: his manufacturing plants, his home and his property in the country. On paper, he looked good. The problem was he had little in the way of cash. Much of his business was done on credit, and his personal bank account had only a few hundred dollars in it when the stock market crashed in 1929. Creditors demanded money. Stock holders cashed in their shares. Bankers closed out loans. In all the chaos, William McLaughlin sat in the den of his great house, placed the muzzle of a revolver in his mouth and ended his problems.

His widow sold the house and moved to a smaller one in Moline with her son. The big house changed hands over time, until it became a rental property in the 1990s.

Everett and Maggie VanHolt moved into the McLaughlin mansion in 1991. It was a huge home for just the two of them. Their sons had both graduated college and moved away in the last few years. The boys were married now, and had lives of their own. Mom and Dad felt more than a little useless.

So Ev and Maggie talked it over and decided they had love left to share. They became foster parents in the summer of '91.

Before the first child moved in, Maggie noticed that odd things went on in the house. The title to their truck disappeared for several weeks, only to re-appear on the kitchen table. Another time, the burners on the gas stove popped on by themselves. Ev checked the switches and cleaned the ignition system.

Then the first three children arrived and distracted them from the strange goings on. Nick, Rick, and Angie were siblings in a bad situation. Authorities had decided that their mom was no longer of capable of caring for them. She was given time to straighten her life up before the kids could go back home with her.

In the meantime, the children would try to move on with their lives as best they could. They brought things from home to make them feel safe. Rick brought his Teddy Bear, Nick brought his cars, and Angie brought her Barbies. They were together at least, and the VanHolts were good people. The kids had a clean, vermin free home for the first time they could remember. They ate three solid meals each day and played in a safe place. They enjoyed their new life. Still, they did miss their mom.

At one point, Rick mentioned that a green light had moved in the hall and scared his Teddy. Maggie had seen it, too. She didn't want to scare the kids, however, and said it was her flashlight as she went to use the bathroom in the night.

Another time, everyone was sitting at the kitchen table eating their lunch, and all heard heavy footsteps in the upstairs hall. They were the only ones in the house. Ev was at work. Maggie felt the goosebumps rise on her skin but didn't want the kids to see, so she made the joke that the cat needed to lose weight.

"Ev," Maggie said that night as they lay in bed. "You think there's something going on with this house?"

"What do you mean?" Ev asked.

"You know, the odd things: the lights, the bed shaking. Today the kids and I heard someone walking around up here."

"Who was it?"

"Ev, you know there isn't anyone else here. I'm being serious."

"Maggie, your Irish is running away with you. Everything has an explanation."

"Really? Explain it to me then. I'd like a way to fix the problem."

"Not tonight. I'm too tired." Ev rolled over to sleep.

"That's what I thought. Go to sleep, Everett."

Next morning, Maggie got the kids up. The two oldest would be off to school. Rick stayed home. Next year he would be in kindergarten. Maggie made breakfast and packed bag lunches for Nick and Angie.

She loaded them into the car, and all went to the school a few blocks away. Nick and Angie stepped out of the car and joined their friends as they walked up the steps to go to class. Maggie went to run a few errands.

Maggie unloaded the groceries at home while Rick went in to play. She put everything away then started on the breakfast dishes. Rick watched his morning shows while he played. His old brown Teddy sat on the couch and watched.

At noon Ev came in for lunch. He had been rewiring a house not far from home, so rather than go to a fast food joint, he decided to come home for a sandwich. Maggie put a meal together for all of them as she and Ev caught up on the day.

A scream from the living room shattered the quiet. Rick ran into the kitchen with his Teddy clutched to his chest. Tears flowed down his flushed cheeks. Blood was smeared across his face.

"Ricky, baby what's wrong?" Maggie leaned over the child. "What happened?"

"Muh- My Teddy." Ricky sobbed. "He's hurt!"

"What?" Ev asked.

Ricky eased the stuffed bear away from his chest. "He cut his ear. It's bleeding."

Maggie looked at the worn bear. His left ear was covered in large gouts of blood. "Ricky, are you hurt?"

"No, Mommy, my bear."

"Can't be," Ev said. He turned the child to face him. With a handkerchief he began to wipe blood from Ricky's face.

"Let me see Bear, Ricky," Maggie said. She took the toy and began to wash the blood from its ear. As soon as she did, it bled again. "Ev, this thing *is* bleeding."

Ev got the blood wiped away from Ricky's face. He looked at his handkerchief, and the blood was gone. There was no more blood on Ricky. It was gone from his shirt and hands. He stuck his head into the living room. There was nothing on the couch or floor.

"Maggie, is that thing…?"

Maggie looked down at the bear. The blood stopped. In seconds, the crimson stream faded, then disappeared all together. Not even a stain was left of the bear.

"No. It's gone." Maggie handed the stuffed animal to the distraught child. "See Ricky, he's all better now. No more hurt."

She gathered the child in her arms, sat in one of the kitchen chairs and snuggled him in her arms until he stopped crying. "Okay, Everett, explain that one to me."

"Can't," Everett said. "I'm a believer."

(Author's note: The McLaughlin house was a real home. My parents live there in the 1990's. The history of the home is fictionalized. It was, in fact, built by an E.L. Smith, and was a frequent stop on the Underground Railroad. According to my mom, the event described above actually happened while she and Dad were foster parents. I witnessed far too many events in that home to mention in this book, including a full body apparition. The house burned to the ground in 1997. My parents were living in Nevada at the time. The day it burned, Mom suddenly felt the presence of the spirit from the McLaughlin house, and a gust of wind blasted through the house and slammed doors. All the windows were closed and locked.)

Down in the Valley

Spring Valley, Illinois, was built by two things: Water passages and coal mines. The industries worked well together. Coal was mined from the hills surrounding the Illinois River Valley, taken to barges on the Illinois and Michigan canal and floated up to Chicago from there. In the Windy City, the coal powered industry and heated homes.

Like most coal mines, the ones in and around Spring Valley relied on immigrant labor. Newcomers from Lithuanian and Poland settled in the valley and quickly found work. In 1914, the Lithuania Liberty Cemetery was incorporated on a high hill in a wooded section of Spring Valley.

Monique Millani sat on the front porch of her house, knees drawn up, arms folded over them, chin resting on top. Her friends Jenny Cattani and Josh Nyzwarski sprawled on the wicker couch and a chair.

"I'm bored," Monique said. She swatted a mosquito. Muggy nights drew the blood suckers up from the backwaters of the Illinois River for their nightly feeds.

"Join the club," Josh said. He flicked a stray stucco rock across the porch.

"What do you want to do?" Jenny asked.

"I'm open to suggestions," Monique said as she stared off down the street.

"C'mon. It's summer break, and none of us has to be in early to work tomorrow," Jenny said. "There's got to be something we can do."

"We could go see the crypt," Monique said.

"YOU could go see the crypt," Josh said. "I ain't going."

"C'mon, chickenshit," Jenny said. "Big strong football player like you is scared of an old rock tomb?"

"That one I am. Place's frakking creepy."

"C'mon. We're going." Monique stood up. She jumped down the steps and hopped into the driver's seat of Josh's truck. She pushed in the clutch and turned the key.

"Hey, you can't drive a stick," Josh shouted. Monique ground the gears in response. "Cut that out."

"Come and drive then." Monique smiled.

With a snarl, Josh walked to the truck. Jenny jumped into the bed as Monique set the brake and slid over.

"Someday I'm going to stop letting your ass tell me what to do," Josh grumbled.

"Oh you love it." Monique laughed.

They drove out the winding streets west of Spring Valley. Thick woods closed in on the narrow blacktop as it snaked through the ravines and hills. At the Y in the road, Josh took the left fork and the truck growled up the hill. Halfway to the top, he swung wide and turned into the tiny lane for the graveyard.

The crypt stared out at them, stone silent to the events it had witnessed for nearly 100 years. The family's name was carved deep into the limestone above the concrete door. Other stones were crowded into the narrow tract of hilltop. Many were written in Lithuanian or Polish.

Red paint someone had splashed on the door shone brightly in the headlights. Monique shuddered. Despite her cockiness, the place scared her, too. Jenny banged on the back window and the two inside jumped.

"We getting out or what?" Jenny asked.

Josh turned off the truck and set the brake. "Yeah," he whispered. "Let's do this."

Headlights from the truck flooded the small graveyard with yellow light. As they walked toward the crypt, long shadows reached ahead of them. To their right, a raccoon chittered as he scratched his way up a tree.

Jenny climbed the two steps to the door. "It's warm," she said as she laid her hand on the concrete slab.

"Course it's warm, idiot. It's eighty degrees out here," Monique said.

"No. I mean it's warmer than the air. Feel it." Jenny ran her hand across the front of the crypt.

Monique reached out a hand. Her fingertips shook. She clenched her fist for a moment, then brushed the front of the vault with the tips of her fingers. "Shit, it *is* warmer."

As they stood on the landing, the three ran their hands across the smooth limestone and concrete.

"Has to be from the sun beating on it all day," Josh said. The front faces south. It gets sun all day."

"Sun's been down for three hours. Ought to be cool by now," Monique argued.

Josh grunted. He reached into his pocket and pulled out his folding knife. "Let me try something."

"Josh, what the hell are you doing?" Jenny asked.

"Just let me try this. They say something is in there."

"Yeah, right," Monique said. She backed down a step. "What are you going to do?"

"Watch," Josh said. With the butt of the handle, he tapped three times on the door. From inside came three taps. They all backed off the steps.

"What was that?" Jenny gasped. "You plan that?"

"Hell, no!" Josh said.

"Then what the hell was it?" Monique said.

"Hell if I know." Josh took a step back.

The lights cut out on his truck, all three screamed. They spun to get to the truck. Five steps later Jenny turned, and screamed again.

"What's that?" She grabbed Monique by the arm and yanked her around.

An orange glow oozed from the front of the crypt. It shimmered for a moment, then formed into a large sphere.

The girls screamed again, turned, and ran for the truck. Josh beat them there, yanked the door to the cab open and jumped in. "Go, Josh, go," Jenny screamed.

Josh smashed the key into the ignition. The engine rolled over slowly, then died. He hit the key again. It rolled over faster, but still wouldn't fire. The orange sphere came toward them, rose up, and landed on the hood of the truck.

"Screw this," Josh said. He popped the emergency brake, threw in the clutch, and let the truck roll backward. The glow clung to the hood. The truck gained speed as they rolled down the hill. He flung his arm over the seat and craned his neck behind to see.

He dodged a tombstone, picked up more speed, and dumped the clutch. The engine coughed, sputtered and roared into life. The sphere moved up the hood.

"Hang on!" Josh shouted. He backed the truck toward the gate.

Monique grabbed his arm. "Hurry, Josh. Get us out of here!"

Josh steered the truck between the gateposts. A loud growl came from the sphere, followed by the shriek of metal. He snapped the wheel to the right, found first gear and dumped the clutch. He rowed through the gears until they blasted along the narrow road into town.

"What the hell was that?" Jenny asked repeatedly like a skipping CD.

"No clue," Monique said. "Not a friggin' clue."

"I ain't goin' back." Josh said. "I ain't goin' back."

At Monique's house, Josh shut the truck off in the driveway. The motion sensor light came on, as they sat for long seconds. After an eternity, Jenny popped her door and stepped out. She moved like an old woman. Josh opened his door and they walked around to the front of the truck.

"What was that scraping sound as we backed out?" Monique asked.

"Branches, I guess." Josh said.

"I don't think so," Jenny said.

82

She pointed to the truck. Two sets of five scratch marks ran down the hood from the window to the front edge. The blue oval in the center of the grill was chipped. Paint was gone from the middle all the way to bare metal.

"Shit," Josh whispered.

Monique vomited into the yard. They went into the house, and locked the doors.

(Author's Note: The Lithuanian Liberty Cemetery was incorporated on a wooded hill in Spring Valley, IL in 1914. The family mausoleum is the biggest structure in the small cemetery. Three brothers are entombed inside. At one point in the 1960s someone broke in and stole a head from one of the bodies. The head was found and returned to its proper resting place. Stories, including the one above, have circulated about the crypt for many years. Some friends at work told me of the place, and I drove over to do a little investigation of my own. While nothing overly creepy happened, I did find that the east wall of the tomb was much warmer than the rest of the structure. I went on a sunny day in Feb. 2007 when it was ten degrees below zero. The east wall was decidedly warmer than the other three. It was mid afternoon, and I could fathom no reason for this. The interlocking limestone blocks were warmer than the blocks they linked to in the other walls. I also noted that while there was snow on the roof and stuck to the west wall, there was none on the east. I would like to go back with a laser heat gauge to get some accurate readings so I can record some scientific results.)

Help Me

The sister towns of Sterling and Rock Falls, Illinois grew up on the Rock River in the 1800s. Industry and farming combined in an area that is centered in the state and an easy reach for commerce going anywhere else. Industries that need a constant, steady supply of water found a home here. Northwest Wire and Steel in Sterling was the largest employer in both cities for decades.

When the Hennepin Canal was built in the early 1900s, farmers in the center of the state were concerned that their wells would be drained from feeding the canal. To stave off the thereat, engineers tapped the Rock River as a source. A forty-mile-long feeder canal was dug from Rock Falls to connect with the Hennepin Canal. So the canal could be fed by three rivers, the Illinois, the Mississippi and the Rock. Of the three, only the Rock is non-navigable by commercial traffic. It does, however, draw hundreds of thousands of people each year for recreation along its length. Fishermen work the waters for Walleye and Bass. Ski boats race through the wider sections of river, and people swim along the shores.

Josie Ramirez walked the path along the river with her boyfriend, Chris Jones, late one evening. The river rolled along quietly until it boiled over the roller of the hydroelectric dam a few blocks to the west. They talked softly, as lovers do, arms around one another's waist.

"Wait, you hear that?" Chris asked.

"Hear what?" Josie said.

"Hold on." Chris stopped and turned an ear toward the Rock. "Sounds like someone is out there."

"What?" Josie listened, too. She could see no lights from a boat, nor hear any engine noise. The only thing she heard was the river as it flowed by.

Ever so faintly something reached her ears. "Help me." The words drifted across the water. "Mommy, help me."

"Somebody out there?" Chris hollered.

"Hello!" Josie shouted. "Where are you?"

"Mommy, help me," the voice called again.

"Can you see anything, Chris?"

Chris pointed toward the middle of the river. "Way out, I think. That little dark spot on the water. Is that a kid's head?"

"Maybe."

"Danny? Where are you, Danny?" A woman's voice cried from the shore up stream from them.

"Mommy, help me. The water's cold."

"Danny, hold on! Mommy's coming."

"Hold on, Danny. I'm calling the rescue squad." Chris flipped his cell phone open. "Jo, go find the mother, I'll go up on the hill in and meet the cops."

"Okay." Josie picked her way up the dark riverbank. "Ma'am, my boyfriend is calling the police. They'll be here soon."

"Danny, swim to shore, baby!" the woman shouted.

"Mommy! Help!" The voice was weaker now, fading.

"Hold on, Danny!" Josie shouted. "Help is coming." A little ways from her, she saw a dark form standing at the edge of the water. "Ma'am," she said reaching out to touched the woman's shoulder.

The woman turned to face Josie, who gasped and crossed herself as she backed away. A black, empty hole filled the space that should have been the woman's face. As Josie watched in horror, the women disappeared.

Chris was there. With him was a city police officer. The cop explained that they got calls now and then about a little boy named Danny who was sucked over the roller dam thirty years ago as his mother watched.

The New House

Geneseo, Illinois, is a farming and industrial community. Elegant Victorian homes are common in the old sections of town. Most have been maintained to such standards that they are in as good a condition now as they were a hundred years ago when they were built.

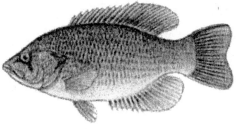

Recreation in the area revolves around the Hennepin Canal. Hiking, rides on horseback along the old towpaths, or putting a boat in and wetting a line for some trout or bass bring people to this part of the canal as long as the ice is out.

Francine VanDerWalle put her briefcase together before she headed to her job for the day. Her husband, Bill, was already at work. He had taken a position with the Illinois Department of Natural Resources and was stationed down the road a few miles in Sheffield. He had grown up in Geneseo, and jumped at the chance to come home and work.

Frankie spent her day at the office filing reports and working on claims. Insurance work swings between tedium and hilarity. Unfortunately, today was simply tedious with paperwork. By five, she was more than ready to go home.

As her key hit the lock in the door, Frankie heard something in the basement. She paused for a moment, cocked her head, and listened. The cat wove his way between her legs as she tried to figure out what she had heard. After a moment, she walked over and opened the door to the cellar.

With an exasperated sigh, she walked downstairs to turn off the washer. Bill must have been home and set a load to run. Frankie opened the lid to find nothing but water in the drum. Now she was irritated. She would have to let the machine run through its cycle with nothing in it so she could do another load. Bill wasn't that forgetful, was he? And just where was he? She didn't see his truck around.

An hour later, Bill showed up. He was muddy to the waist, and his shirt was liberally smeared with mud and duckweed. Frankie met him at the door. She picked a small chunk of moss off his face with a giggle.

"What'd you do? Fall in the canal?" Frankie said, smiling.

Bill slid out of his boots. He dropped his pants. "No, the marsh off the canal at Hennepin. We cleaned duck boxes all day."

"Aw, you poor thing," Frankie said. "Take all that stuff out back and hose it off. We'll throw it in the wash."

Bill headed out the back door for the spigot. Frankie turned. "Hey, Bill, is this the first time you've been home?"

"Since this morning, yes. Why?" Bill picked another string of moss from his ear.

"No reason. I came home and the washer was going."

"You must have left it running this morning then."

"Yeah, must have."

Frankie thought for a moment. She couldn't have left it on this morning and have it still running eight hours later. No, that couldn't be it.

Life continued. Insurance claims were filed. Work was done on the Hennepin. They spent time together in the yard and went out with friends on the weekends. On the holidays, their kids came home from college.

Still, odd things happened in the house. Again the washer came on. This time while they both did dishes in the kitchen sink. Bill explained it away by blaming the wiring in the house. It was built in 1895, and nobody knew when it had been wired. Just old wiring. Same as for when the TV blinked on and off in the middle of the night. Frankie got in the habit of unplugging the set before they went to bed.

One night late in the fall, they lay in bed wrapped around one another. Deer season started in the morning, and they would be up soon to rush in the woods with their bows.

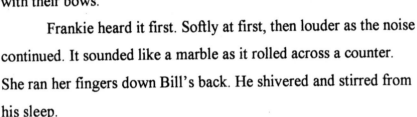

Frankie heard it first. Softly at first, then louder as the noise continued. It sounded like a marble as it rolled across a counter. She ran her fingers down Bill's back. He shivered and stirred from his sleep.

"What, Honey?"

"Listen," Frankie said.

The rolling sound continued. It got louder, then something clattered to the floor. Bill reached over and flipped on his bedside light. There on the floor was one of Frankie's lipsticks. The top was off. As they watched, it rotated until the color showed from the top of the tube. It turned until it was extended all the way. Frankie reached out to pick it up. She paused for a moment, then gathered it up with trembling fingers.

"I told you something weird was going on in this house." She said as she held the tube up.

"Okay. You're right. I just can't explain it, that's all. So now what do we do?"

"I say we go deer hunting and try to figure out the next step. When we get home, we should call the pastor and have him come out and bless the house."

"Sounds like a plan," Bill said.

Frankie put her lipstick away, careful to run it all the way down before putting the cap on. A week later, they had their pastor come for dinner and bless the house. From then on, there were few things that went bump in the night.

At the Picture Show

Princeton, Illinois, sits in the middle of the state. It is a quiet little town, with a combination of antique and crafts shops mixed with industry that bring people here to settle. Only a few miles south, the Hennepin Canal draws many residents out to fish and hike. The slow-moving waters are ideal for small boats or canoes.

Princeton is an old prairie town, established in the early 1800s. Men from the area took part in the Black Hawk Wars, and some of the outlying areas endured attacks by the Sac and Fox tribes. Abraham Lincoln fought with his militia in this area and mustered out a few miles east, in Oglesby.

Princeton grew, and by the early 1900s was a thriving town. It was fed by commerce from both the railroads, and the Hennepin Canal. Downtown did a brisk business in everything from medicines to horseless carriages.

Thomas Smyth decided that business was so good he opened an Opera House in 1910. For a few years, Smyth booked live performances on the grand stage. Vaudeville acts came through, with an occasional orchestra. Then moving pictures came to town, and Smyth could see where the future was, so he converted grand stage into two movie theaters.

Dan Fogleson unlocked the door to the theater early one Wednesday morning. The city was just beginning to wake. The coffee shop next door started its morning rush as people stopped in on the way to work for their shot of jitter juice.

The new movies for the week sat inside the doors in their sealed cans. Dan set his briefcase on the ticket counter, collected the films, and put them in the office. It was strange they were inside the lobby. There was a lock box outside the door for the new reels to go in. The person who delivered the films had a key to the box. It was odd they weren't there. With a shrug, he gathered his papers for the day and went to work.

Pat MacManus, the owner, had asked Dan to take over the management of the Opera House. New multiplex theaters in towns nearby threatened to force the old place to close. Dan started with small renovations: new light bulbs in the marquee, fresh paint in the lobby, and new material on the walls.

Dan opened the doors for the painters that morning. They would finish the small lobby and move on to the two screening rooms in the next two days.

"Hey, Dan," the head painter stuck his head into the office. "You got someone in here?"

"No, Jack, I just unlocked."

"That's strange. You better come here." Jack scratched the stubble on his chin.

"What's wrong?" Dan stood from his desk and followed the painter. In the foyer to the first screening room was a red handprint on the wall. Long rivulets ran from the print. The trim was to be done in red, while the walls were to be done in off-white. The walls were done, trim was all that was left.

"Well, it's still wet," Jack said. "We'll wipe off what we can and paint over it. You've had somebody in here though."

"Yeah, the guy that delivers movies was here last night. I'll have to talk to him about it."

"Do that. Red's a pain to paint over. It never covers well."

Jack and his crew did the repair and finished their job. Faintly under the new coat of white, the red hand bled through. Not much, but if one looked close, it was there. Jack put two coats of primer on it and two more of finish. He didn't want to put more on it, he told Dan, because it would affect the sheen of the finish coat.

A week later, Dan was at the theater when the movies were delivered. The young man with the reels dropped them in the box as Dan came out of his office. He denied putting the movies inside last week and painting the wall. Didn't even have a key to the door, he said. He offered Dan to check his keychain, which Dan did without finding one to his front door. He apologized to the young man, and they concluded there must have been a break in.

Pat came in later that day to check on things. Dan told him about the paint and movies when it happened. He explained to his boss that the delivery man didn't have a key.

"I'll let you in on something, Dan," Pat said. He sat on the edge of the desk as he drank his coffee from the little shop. "Strange things happen here. People see things. Money envelopes move to a different drawer five minutes after we're done with the count. Projectors come on when no one's around to run them."

Dan grinned a little sideways. "You tellin' me this place is haunted."

Pat grinned. "I'm just saying strange things happen."

They moved on to other business. Bills were made out and payroll had to be met. Afterward, Dan pretty much forgot about what Pat had told him. There had to be a logical explanation for things, maybe an ex-employee had a key or something. He'd have to figure it out.

A few weeks later, Dan was setting up a new movie in the projector. Shelia, the girl who ran the machine when they showed movies, helped him thread the film through. Only the film booth was lighted. To their  right was a door that led into the old balcony. These seats were used back when the theater still booked live acts. It had been walled off back in the 1950s when the building had been renovated for nothing but movies.

Sheila went into the balcony to get a screwdriver from the toolbox they kept up there. The old projector had a few quirks, and sometimes parts needed to be tightened for it to work right. She left the door open as she came back through it.

Dan glanced up from their work. "Hey, who's that?" He nodded towards the balcony.

"Who's who?" Sheila asked

"That guy in there."

Sheila turned. In the second row sat a young man, his back to them, as he stared out at where the screen would be. He was dressed in a white tee shirt and blue jeans. "Hey buddy," Sheila said. "You ain't supposed to be up here."

"How the hell did he get in here?" Dan asked.

"I don't know. Hey buddy…."

Shelia screamed as the young man disappeared. Dan dropped the screwdriver, walked to the door in two strides, and slammed it closed.

"C'mon, I'll stand you an espresso." Dan left the room at a fast walk, Shelia at his heels.

Word slowly got around to what they had seen. One day, as Dan sat at the counter of the coffee shop, Ed Jones, the unofficial historian of Princeton, approached him. He told Dan the theater had been haunted for better than fifty years. Before the balcony was walled off, a young man leaned over the rail to talk to his friends in the rows below. The rail gave way, and he fell twenty feet to his death. Since then, he's been there to play tricks and scare people.

On HELP Road

Ottawa, Illinois, is a pretty little town on the banks of the Illinois River. The newer parts of town climb the bluffs on either side of the river valley. Stores and homes nestle into the rock of the valley walls, while ancient trees keep watch.

Behind the High School, the Fox River empties into the Illinois. With all the water in town, it was a natural that the Illinois and Michigan Canal would come through Ottawa. Trade on the canal and the rivers grew the town from a collection of tents and small wooden structures, to a thriving community by the middle 1800s. Many who worked on the canal settled in town and added their skills to everyday life.

As Ottawa grew, other means of transportation added to the town's growth. Interstate 80 was laid out to pass just north of town. New business populated that section of town. The metropolis became a good blend of the old and new.

One of the new businesses is the Silver Slipper Gentleman's Club right off Interstate 80. The girls are friendly and the beer is cold. It's a good place to go if a body is inclined to find a place to get away from life for a while.

"Hi, Jim," said the pretty blond. "Mind if sit?"

The man looked up from his notebook. "Depends," he said. "Am I talking to Candy tonight, or Beth?"

The blond sat in the empty chair at his little round table. "Oh, for goodness sakes. With you, I'm always Beth."

"Unless you're naked in my lap."

She smiled. "That's just kinky Beth."

"Ah. You want some coffee?"

"Been a long night, I could use some."

Jim excused himself to the bar for a few minutes to retrieve the java. Beth pulled the notebook to her side of the table and glanced through it. She returned it as Jim handed her the mug.

"If you were anyone else, I'd get pissed at you looking through my notes." Jim pulled the chair under him.

"Writer's block sucks, don't it?" Beth took a sip of the coffee and made a face. "I wish Lou would learn to make a decent pot."

"Hell, it's probably been sitting there for three hours."

"Yeah, and he strains the grounds through our stockings."

They both laughed. Jim loved to make her laugh. The sound was music in his hears. With him, it was never faked. She was Beth. The same girl he went to high school with and occasionally shared a bed with. It had been the same for the past eight years. Since he came back from college and found her here one night when he was trying to work out his writer's block. She had found a number of ways to eliminate his tension that first night, and it became his habit to bring his notebook now.

"So, what is it you're stuck on?" Beth folded her hands in front if her and rested her chin on them.

"Aw, my editor has me working on a story about local legends. I'm stuck for something interesting." Jim chewed on his pen as he watched another blond by the name of Star twirl and wiggle around the stage.

Beth tapped his arm. "I'm over here."

"Sorry. Plenty of distractions. Like I was saying, I'm having trouble thinking of something to write about."

"How about HELP road?"

"What's that?"

"That's right, you were away at Southern when it happened." Beth took another sip from her mug.

"So spill."

"I'll do better. I'll take you out there after work." She stood and took his hand. "C'mon."

"You're not off shift yet."

"No, I'm not. Kinky Beth wants to give her favorite reporter a lap dance on the house."

Jim grinned. "I like kinky Beth."

They shared a lingering kiss before she led him upstairs.

At two thirty, Beth came around from the back dressed in her civvies: A pair of blue jeans and a grey sweatshirt. It was spring, so there was a nip in the air. Her hair was pulled back in a ponytail. A small purse was slung over her shoulder.

"You're messing with my man, Star," Beth said with a smile. She laid her hand on the younger dancer's shoulder.

Star looked up at her friend and smiled sweetly. "Didn't know you owned him, Candy."

"He's mine; he just won't admit it."

"Excuse me, girls, do I have a say in this?" Jim asked.

"No," they replied in unison.

"Great. Well, since I don't have a say in this, and you own me these days, shouldn't we get going, Beth?" Jim stood and held out his arm. Beth slid hers into it as they left the club.

They climbed into Jim's truck, and he turned north out of the lot. Less than a mile up, he turned west onto a narrow county blacktop. Beth explained that twelve years past, a biker left the little bar halfway down this road. He was drunk and didn't know the road well. He blew a curve going pretty fast and he and his girlfriend got hurt. The man climbed out of the ditch, and wrote "HELP" on the road with his blood. Then he crawled back in the ditch with his girlfriend, and they both died.

"Sounds like a bad wreck," Jim said. "Don't know that it's enough to make a story out of."

"Well, here's where your story comes in," Beth said. "An old farmer found them next morning and called the cops. The sheriff came out. They did the whole report and investigation thing and cleaned up. Scrubbed the road where the blood was. Next morning, the same farmer came back the same way, and there was "HELP" written on the road again. Cops came out and scrubbed it off with chemicals this time. It was gone for a while, but it still comes back from time to time."

"Sounds like an urban legend. Where's this wreck site?"

"Keep driving, but take it easy. We don't want to become part of this spook story."

Jim eased off the gas as they dropped down over a long hill. The Fox River ran through the bottom of the valley, with a small hydro-electric plant built into it at this point. Halfway up the hill on the other side was a small tavern, closed now after the owner died. The biker left the lot and headed west. Jim followed the route.

As the hill topped out, it began to wind. Curves made the road dangerous. Jim slowed even more to keep the truck from sliding. At one point they went into a long straight stretch, and he started to put his foot in the gas. Beth laid a hand on his arm and told him not to, the curve was close.

Jim slowed more. He crept along, barely over 30, when the road cut right in a tight-banked curve. Halfway into the curve, he brought the truck to a full stop. "HELP" glistened on the pavement in front of them.

"Cute, Beth."

"What?" Her blue eyes shown wide in the dim light from the dash.

"You set this up."

"How could I set this up? I didn't know you were coming in tonight."

Jim could feel her shake as she leaned into him. "It's okay. Someone's out here pulling a prank then. C'mon." He reached into his glovebox and pulled out his digital camera and flashlight. His steno notebook was in his hip pocket.

"Jim, don't go out there. Something ain't right."

"It's okay, baby." Jim gave her a soft hug, then slid out.

"Wait. You're not leaving me in here alone." Beth hopped out. She stood beside Jim as he crouched near the ragged message. He reached out a finger. "Jim, don't," she said.

He smiled up at her over the rims of his glasses. "It's okay, Beth." Jim dipped the tip of his finger into the stain and rubbed it between that and his thumb. "Fresh."

Jim stood and wiped the blood on a handkerchief in his back pocket. He stood and snapped a few frames with his camera. "Look." He pointed to the corner of the "P." There were spatters of blood and partial handprints that led from there into the ditch. He shot some frames of that as well, then headed for the grass.

"Jimmy, don't, I'm telling you, something isn't right here."

Jim flicked on the light, and followed the trail into the weeds. Beth clung to his shirt. There, in the long grass, a shattered motorcycle lay on its side. The smell of gas was strong. A woman sprawled not far away, her head twisted back, a ugly bulge in the side of her neck. A man lay face-down beside her, an arm draped over her body.

"Lord, someone is taking this joke too far," Jim muttered. From behind, Beth let out a little whimper as he stepped into the ditch. He crouched down beside the man, and laid a hand on his shoulder. "Okay, buddy. Joke's over. You've had your sick laugh."

Jim rolled the man onto his back, but the man's intestines stayed in a pile where they were. Jim swore and sat back. Beth gasped and started to say something but was cut off as the man grabbed Jim's wrist.

"Help us, please." the man groaned.

"Jesus!" Jim jerked his arm in surprise, but the man held fast. "Let go, Mister, I'll call the cops for you."

"Help us," he moaned again.

Jim tried to pull his arm away, but the man had hold of his wrist like a steel trap. "Damnit, Mister. Let go and I'll call for help."

Beth grabbed the man's arm in order to pull it away. "We'll call someone, sir, but he has to use his cell."

The man sat up. "Help us." Blood sprayed through his lips into his greasy beard. His eyes were white lights in his gaunt, grey face. "Please help. My wife's dying."

Beth let go of the man's arm, crossed herself and scrambled backwards. Jim jerked his arm free, never taking his eyes off the biker's face. He backed up a few feet to sit at the edge of the blacktop.

The man reached out again. "Help us," he said. Then he began to fade. Like an old-fashioned TV set as it was turned off, the entire scene disappeared. First the wrecked bike, then the woman. The man faded last, still reaching out for Jim.

Like a ninety-year-old man, Jim climbed to his feet and stood there shaking. He offered a hand to Beth and pulled her up into his arms. She hung there, limp.

"Stay with me tonight," she whispered.

"I was just going to ask you the same," he replied.

Neither said a word as Jim drove to Beth's house-a clean little two bedroom affair on the bluffs. She paused for a moment as she unlocked the door. Birds were singing. Morning was coming.

Jim pulled off his shirt in the bedroom as Beth slid under the covers. "I guess it really did happen," he said.

"What do you mean?"

Jim held up his arm where the biker grabbed him. A red handprint could be seen in the tan skin of his wrist.

"Lord," Beth whispered. "Come to bed Jim."

"Gladly." Jim slid under the covers. He wrapped Beth in his arms and held her close. The last thing he was aware of before he fell into an exhausted sleep was the rhythm of her soft breathing.

Movie Magic

Tiskilwa, Illinois, is a sleepy little town in the valley of Big Bureau Creek. The town grew up on farms and mills along the creek-bank. Railroads passed through town and brought more commerce. Then the Hennepin Canal came through town and brought not only workers but trade as well.

The Hennepin Canal closed down, but people in the area still use the waterway. Retired farmers and steelworkers gather every morning to drink a pot of coffee at one of the two restaurants in town. From there, they gather their bait and poles and spend the morning at the canal. Others paddle their canoes down this old artery of the state.

Still, the old Victorian mansions watch over the town from the main street, as they have for more than a hundred years. The canal can be seen from the upper story of many of the homes. Their builders often came from Chicago through the canals on weekend retreats. One giant brick structure is well maintained. A large family still calls the place home.

Another large mansion, while still in one piece is not in such good shape. While still livable, the rotted porch, broken upper windows and uninsulated walls make it a less than ideal as a home. It is used as a weekend house, but the new owners are only around as their schedules permit.

They are from Chicago, however, and have friends in the film industry. The Windy City has its own movie industry, in addition to the theater and improv companies. One such moviemaker was a young lady by the name of Tammy Jamison. A film school graduate, she was a new star in the independent film world of Chicago.

Tammy liked to shoot on location, and small towns with an interesting character were something she was on the lookout for.

She found the place for her next film when she spent the weekend with her friends in Tiskilwa.

Throughout the summer, Tammy made trips to town to arrange for everything she needed. Permits were issued. She got permission from the neighbors to use footage in case they or their homes were in background shots. Local actors from the college and high school auditioned for roles. By August, everything was in place to start the shoot.

When the film crew arrived at the old mansion, they were impressed by the gothic look of the old structure. They would shoot a suspense story there in town with local talent.

Things went smoothly for the first week. Actors studied their scripts and practiced with one another. They spent hours in the large front yard or the nearby park as they memorized their lines.

Jane Friel, who was part of the drama group at Illinois Valley Community College, would sit on the weed-choked lawn to study her lines. At times, she could feel someone watching her. The feeling was so strong that sometimes she turned around expecting to see one of the other actors in the yard with her. That wasn't always the case. When no one was there, she would study the house, as if it would speak to her.

Chris Tonazzi sat with her one morning, as she and Jane worked on their lines. Jane glanced up at the house. The hairs rose on the back of her neck. Chris followed the look.

"Jane, I have to ask you something," Chris said.

With some difficulty, Jane dragged her attention back to her script. "Where were we?" she asked.

"Jane!"

"What?" Jane glanced up, startled.

"I need to know something."

"What? We have lines to run."

"This is more important than lines." Chris looked around her, then leaned close to her friend. "Has anything weird happened to you in this house?"

"Define weird." Jane looked across the street. The pizza place would be open for lunch soon. Maybe she would take a break over there this afternoon....

"Besides how you're behaving right now?" Chris took Jane gently by the wrist. "Look, I've felt someone touch me in an empty room in that house. My hair has flipped when the closest person is twenty feet away. That place is not normal."

"I feel like I'm always being watched. Even in the middle of a scene, I can feel eyes on me." Jane turned to look at the house. "Upstairs is the worst."

"God, I'm glad I'm not the only one."

Tammy called for them at that moment. The next scene was set up. They were ready. Chris and Jane took their scripts and headed upstairs, careful not to trip over all the wires strung like colorful snakes across the floor.

Chris hit her mark in the upstairs hall as the cameras began to roll. Jane waited for her to get closer to the door of the bedroom she stood in before she would enter the scene. As Chris crept closer, Jane tensed. She knew her lines, she knew how she wanted to work the scene out. They had gone over this part of the production for two days.

Jane waited as Chris passed. She opened the door slowly, so as to step into the room quietly. As she made her move, Jane felt a hand hit the middle of her back, and shove her into the hall. With a yelp of surprise, she stumbled into the hall.

She caught a glimpse of an old man dressed in a red plaid shirt with black suspenders that held up his blue jeans. Jane started to say something about ruining her entrance, when the old man slammed the door.

"Who the hell was that guy?" Jane asked. "We weren't supposed to have anyone else in the scene."

"We didn't have anyone else in the room." Tammy said. "Go check it."

Together they walked into the room. They shouted for the man to come out. Asked who he was. Told him he needed to come out and leave the shoot. They got no reply. The bedroom was on the second floor, and there was no way out, save past the entire crew. As they searched, they found nothing but an empty room.

No one could figure out how he had disappeared. One of the cameramen called Tammy over as she stepped back into the hall. He backed his footage up to the point where Chris walked past the room. As she passed, Jane flew into the hall. Framed in the door briefly, was a pulsating black shadow. Around the edges, white light crackled. Jane whirled to say something to the shadow, and the door slammed in her face.

"What was that?" Jane whispered. She ran her hands over her arms to still the goosebumps that raced over her skin. "Tell me you jacked with the camera."

"No, ma'am," The cameraman replied. "I just ran this back while you guys were checking the room."

"What was that, Robert?" Tammy asked.

"I don't know, boss. We all saw that old man. I run it back, I get this shadow. You tell me what it is."

"Okay. I'm calling a two hour break. You guys go have a coffee or a beer or whatever," Tammy said. "Get your heads together, and we'll try it again later. Robert, save that footage to a disc. It'll make for some interesting conversation."

"What about you?" Robert asked.

"I'll be okay. I'm going to get me some coffee down at the tavern. Maybe I'll get the priest from the church and have him come in for a visit."

Talk to the Reaper

Sammi Hansen lived in Ottawa, Illinois, all of her life. She lived there because her family had lived there all the way back to the time that the Illinois and Michigan canal was dug through the area. Johan Hansen emigrated to Illinois from Denmark in the 1830s. He crossed his new country by foot. When he got to the Prairie State, he put down roots in a small town on the shores of Lake Michigan by the name of Chicago.

After he finished work on the I and M Canal, he settled in Ottawa with the sister of one of his Irish co-workers. Their family grew and stayed in the valley.

Sammi was seventh generation to live there. She graduated from high school, went to the community college down the road, and opened her own small business in Ottawa. Her coffee shop overlooked the river. People could come in, have a cup of coffee and log onto their computer. A growing number of people in town did an electronic commute to Chicago daily.

Her mother came in to work with her on occasion. For two reasons: To help Sammi cut down on business cost and simply to have someone to talk to. Most days it was no problem for Kate. She had little to do at home beside yard work. Her husband, Frank, had died when Sammi was in grade school. Kate lived on her income from selling real estate in the afternoons and weekends.

The two women washed dishes in the large slop sink at the back of the kitchen one morning after the early rush. Only two customers sat at computer terminals with mugs.

"Sammi, I've been having some weird intuitions the last few nights," Kate said as she ran a plate into the sterilizing sink.

"Mom, they're just bad dreams."

"No, not these. These are the ones that are more."

"You have two different types of dream?"

"Always have, and you know it. Probably you do yourself, you just won't admit it. Too much of your father's Danish in you."

Sammi sighed and handed her mother another dish. "Yeah, and your Irish runs away with you too often. Okay. I'll bite. What're the dreams about?"

"I don't know. I can't put a finger on it, but it feels like death." Kate put the plate in a rack to dry.

Sammi turned with a furrowed brow. "What do you mean death?" There were times she wished she were more like her Dad, but her Mom's superstition did come out on occasion.

"Death. Someone is going to die, but I don't know who."

"Lord, Mom. You're just worried about something. Can we find a subject less morbid?"

"Okay. Who're you dating these days?"

"Mother!"

They went back to work with wide smiles.

As the days went by, Kate became haggard and drawn. She made mistakes where she didn't normally. Sammi noticed it, and pulled her Mom aside for a talk one day. Kate admitted she was still having the dreams, and couldn't shake the feeling that death was close. More, she had become convinced it was her own death she was dreaming of.

"Mom, you have to get past these dreams. Something is stressing you out. Have you talked to anyone? Father Peter would be more than willing to talk I'm sure."

"This is something God is telling me, dear."

"No, He's not. It's some kind of stress that's got you worked up."

"I don't want to discuss this anymore," Kate said. She turned back to the coffee pots.

A week later, Sammi took orders herself all day. Kate had called to say she wouldn't be in. She had an appointment to talk with Father Peter. She came in the next morning, looking much at peace. Sammi was jumpy next to her mother's calm. Something had her on edge, but she couldn't put her finger on it.

She went to the back room to collect some bagels for the lunch rush. No one was in the store, so Kate decorated slender slices of cheesecake.

"Hello, Frank."

Sammi heard her mom as she talked to a customer. Strange she hadn't heard the chimes ring on the door.

"It's good to see you, Katharine."

Sammi could hear the man's voice. A deep, rich, baritone that was familiar but that she couldn't place. She didn't associate the voice with the shop, and she didn't know anyone named Frank who came in regularly.

"I'll come back for you in two days, Katharine."

Sammi peaked around the corner of the door. Come back for her? Her mother hadn't been on a date in fifteen years. Who was this guy?

"I'll see you in two days."

A man turned and walked for the door. He snugged a dark fedora down on his head. He was tall and slender, wearing a dark sports coat and new blue jeans. He looked familiar, with the way he walked, but Sammi still couldn't place him.

"Mother, who was that?" Sammi arched her eyebrow at her mom. Kate hummed a little tune as she turned away.

"An old friend," Kate said.

Sammi waited for more, fists on hips. "That's it? An old friend?"

"That's it." Kate looked up from her cakes. "I want you to know Samantha, that I'm proud of what you've done here, and proud of you as a daughter. A woman couldn't ask for better."

"Mom...."

"Hush now. I'm just being a silly thing."

"Mother, is something wrong?"

"No, Samantha. Everything is right. Now, I have to get back to work."

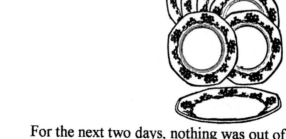

For the next two days, nothing was out of place. Kate was chipper, in a better mood than she'd been in for quite a while.

Sammi stepped into the cooler to fetch some cream cheese. Kate sliced tomatoes for lunch sandwiches.

"It's time, Katharine,"

Sammi heard the same muffled voice as before. She ducked out of the cooler. She could see nothing more than the brim of the dark fedora.

"I'm ready, Frank." Kate looked up at the man. The knife clattered to the floor. She staggered for a moment, held her hand out to catch the edge of the table, missed and fell to the floor.

"Mom!" Sammi dashed to Kate's side.

"I love you, Samantha." Kate's eyes rolled back in her head.

"Mother!" Sammi whirled on the man who still stood behind the counter. "You," She shouted. "You call 911. Get some help out here."

"It is too late. She is with me now."

"What? Who the hell are you?" Sammi looked at the man. His features were out of focus. She couldn't make out what he looked like.

"I am a collector. We look like those we gather want us look like." The man shimmered, began to fade. "I am not here for you. It was Katharine's time. She is safe."

"Screw you," Sammi whispered. She jumped to her feet and grabbed for the telephone at the end of the counter. She punched out 911. As the system rang through, she glanced up. The man was gone. The door hadn't opened; she would have heard the chimes. No one else was in the room. An operator picked up the emergency message. Sammi relayed her emergency and, the operator sent the rescue squad but Kate passed on.

The Old High School

Morris, Illinois, is an older town, not far down the Illinois and Michigan Canal from Chicago. It was one of the first towns to be built by trade from that water route. The old section of town spreads out on either side of the canal and the Illinois River. Storefronts of brick, made in local kilns, line the street.

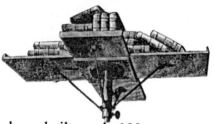

The high school was built nearly 100 years ago, and the town has a long history of success in its many programs. Hundreds of feet below the school, however, is a network of old coal mines that honeycomb the area. The coal was used locally, as well as shipped to Chicago on the I and M Canal.

Chad Culver started his job as the night janitor in the middle of the school year. He had been on the maintenance staff for a few years, and when a position opened on the night shift, Chad put in for the position. Since his had wife left him five years ago, he found it was not an issue to work the odd shift. He could go home at midnight, watch a few shows, and go to bed. During the day, he had time to do things around the house, or make a little extra money doing handyman work in the area.

Before he left, Dan, the retiring janitor, warned him that the school was quite creepy at night. It was something that you never totally got used to. At times, Dan thought his mind would play tricks on him, as he had seen people walking the halls when he knew the place was empty. Chad laughed it off and thanked Dan for the tip.

The first day Chad came in for his new shift, there were several things going on. Basketball practice was in full swing for both the boy's and girl's teams. In the auditorium, students practiced for the Spring Musical that would start a week's run in early March. It was nearly as busy for a few hours in the evening as it was in daylight.

After the last student left, Chad had the place to himself. He had already done a number of his chores, so he decided to polish the floor in a particular stretch of hall. As he walked back to his maintenance area, he noticed how his footsteps echoed in the empty building. He shivered a moment, caught himself and shouted "hello" into the dark. His voiced bounced around and came back to him.

"'ello," the distorted voice said.

Chad gave a small laugh. "Sound like a Brit."

When he got the big polisher back to the hall he wanted to work on, Chad needed to sweep the floor. He didn't want anything to scratch the floor. In a small closet there were a few tools. He retrieved a large red dust mop and began to push it down the hall. It would take three passes to clean the tile.

When he started, all the doors were closed. Halfway down the loop, Chad heard the distinct click of a doorknob as it turned. He glanced up, and one of the doors to the library swung open.

"That's odd." He thought.

He leaned the handle against a locker and went to close it. Chad poked his head inside, found no one, and shut the door. His face reflected in the glass panel. Behind that, he thought he saw the reflection of a woman. He whirled, but there was no one there.

Again the shivers raced down his spine. Chad shook himself, walked back to the dust mop and started his circuit. Nothing else happened while he finished the hall.

With the buffer running, he could hear little. The machine created quite a noise with its motor, let alone the pad that spun under it. At one point, Chad glanced down the hall. Again the door to the library stood open. This time, the light was on.

"Who the hell is in there?" With a sigh, Chad shut down the machine and locked the handle.

He stepped inside the library. Behind the desk stood an older woman, her silver hair pulled back in a bun. She wore an old-fashioned dress, like his grandmother wore in the 1950s. She had on a pair of cat's eye glasses that were jeweled on the sides.

"Ma'am, you're not supposed to be in here," Chad said.

The woman glanced up from her work at him. She put her fingers to her lips to shush him.

"Look, I know this is a library, but you're not supposed to be in here. We could both get in a lot of trouble."

The woman smiled at him, shrugged her shoulders, and disappeared. It was instantly dark as the lights cut out. Chad bit off a scream as he backed out the door and slammed it behind him.

In the hall, Chad collected his tools and raced to his work area. He poured a cup of coffee and sat for a long time. After an hour, he got up, and went to work at the other end of the building.

Later in the year, Chad looked through some old yearbooks. There in the 1958 copy was the librarian he had seen his first night. She had died during the school year of heart failure. After that, he was sure to work on that hall only while people were in the building.

A book doesn't get written by itself. An author doesn't develop in a vacuum. This is especially true for this type of book, and for me as a writer.

Thank you my dear Fay, for putting up with my writing, early hours, and frustrations. I love you for it.

Thank you Trey Barker for being my Solieri, and telling me when I have too many words. Thanks to Jim, Glen, Chris and the rest of the Green River Writer's Group for keeping me honest.

For Cindy Belan, one of my best friends in the world, thank you for the encouragement when I was ready to quit and the laughs when I needed them.

For the people at work who gave me some great stories: Dustin Eckberg and Dustin Hale, Leah Harker, Bill Hahn and Brian Beams. Thanks.

Thank you to Larry Morgenson, for making me get up in class and speak, even when I was terrified to.

To everyone else who told me stories or invited me into their homes to check it out myself. I couldn't have put it all together without all of you.

My Own Ghost Hunting Notes

My Own Ghost Hunting Notes

My Own Ghost Hunting Notes

My Own Ghost Hunting Notes

My Own Ghost Hunting Notes

My Own Ghost Hunting Notes

My Own Ghost Hunting Notes

My Own Ghost Hunting Notes

My Own Ghost Hunting Notes

My Own Ghost Hunting Notes

GHOSTS OF INTERSTATE 90 Chicago to Boston by D. Latham

GHOSTS of the Whitewater Valley by Chuck Grimes

GHOSTS of Interstate 74 by B. Carlson

GHOSTS of the Ohio Lakeshore Counties by Karen Waltemire

GHOSTS of Interstate 65 by Joanna Foreman

GHOSTS of Interstate 25 by Bruce Carlson

GHOSTS of the Smoky Mountains by Larry Hillhouse

GHOSTS of the Illinois Canal System by David Youngquist

GHOSTS of the Niagara River by Bruce Carlson

Ghosts of Little Bavaria by Kishe Wallace

Shown above (at 85% of actual size) are the spines of other Quixote Press books of ghost stories.
These are available at the retailer from whom this book was procured, or from our office at 1-800-571-2665 cost is $9.95 + $3.50 S/H.

GHOSTS of Lookout Mountain by Larry Hillhouse

GHOSTS of Interstate 77 by Bruce Carlson

GHOSTS of Interstate 94 by B. Carlson

GHOSTS of MICHIGAN'S U. P. by Chris Shanley-Dillman

GHOSTS of the FOX RIVER VALLEY by D. Latham

GHOSTS ALONG I-35 by B. Carlson

Ghostly Tales of Lake Huron **by Roger H. Meyer**

Ghost Stories by Kids, for Kids by some really great fifth graders

Ghosts of Door County, Wisconsin by Geri Rider

Ghosts of the Ozarks by B Carlson

Ghosts of US - 63 by Bruce Carlson

Ghostly Tales of Lake Erie by Jo Lela Pope Kimber

GHOSTS OF DALLAS COUNTY   by Lori Pielak

Ghosts of US - 66 from Chicago to Oklahoma   By McCarty & Wilson

Ghosts of the Appalachian Trail   by Dr. Tirstan Perry

Ghosts of I- 70   by B. Carlson

Ghosts of the Thousand Islands   by Larry Hillhouse

Ghosts of US - 23 in Michigan   by B. Carlson

Ghosts of Lake Superior   by Enid Cleaves

GHOSTS OF THE IOWA GREAT LAKES   by Bruce Carlson

Ghosts of the Amana Colonies   by Lori Erickson

Ghosts of Lee County, Iowa   by Bruce Carlson

The Best of the Mississippi River Ghosts   by Bruce Carlson

Ghosts of Polk County Iowa   by Tom Welch

Ghosts of Interstate 75	by Bruce Carlson
Ghosts of Lake Michigan	by Ophelia Julien
Ghosts of I-10	by C. J. Mouser
GHOSTS OF INTERSTATE 55	by Bruce Carlson
Ghosts of US - 13, Wisconsin Dells to Superior	by Bruce Carlson
Ghosts of I-80	David Youngquist
Ghosts of the Cumberland River	by Bruce Carlson
Ghosts of US 550	by Richard DeVore
Ghosts of Erie Canal	by Tony Gerst
Ghosts of the Ohio River	by Bruce Carlson
Ghosts of Warren County	by Various Writers
Ghosts of I-71 Louisville, KY to Cleveland, OH	by Bruce Carlson

Ghosts of Ohio's Lake Erie shores & Islands Vacationland   by B. Carlson

Ghosts of Des Moines County   by Bruce Carlson

Ghosts of the Wabash River   by Bruce Carlson

Ghosts of Michigan's US 127   by Bruce Carlson

GHOSTS OF I-79   *BY BRUCE CARLSON*

Ghosts of US-66 from Ft. Smith to Flagstaff   by Connie Wilson

Ghosts of US 6 in Pennsylvania   by Bruce Carlson

Ghosts of the Missouri River   by Marcia Schwartz

Ghosts of the Tennessee River in Tennessee   by Bruce Carlson

Ghosts of the Tennessee River in Alabama by Bruce Carlson

Ghosts of Pamlico Sound   by Linda June Furr

GHOSTS OF THE BLUE RIDGE PARKWAY   BY LARRY HILLHOUSE

Mysteries of the Lake of the Ozarks   by Hean & Sugar Hardin

GHOSTS OF CALIFORNIA'S STATE HIGHWAY 49   BY MOLLY TOWNSEND

Ghosts of La Salle County   by Joan Kalbacken

Ghosts of Illinois River   by Sylvia Shults

Ghosts of Lincoln Highway in Ohio   by Bruce Carlson

Ghosts of the Susquehanna River   by Bruce Carlson

Ghostly Tales of Route 66: AZ to CA   by Connie Corcoran Wilson

Ghosts of the Natchez Trace   by Larry Hillhouse

Ghosts of Kentucky's Country Music Highway   by Bruce Carlson

Ghosts of Arkansas Highway #7   by Gary Weibye

Ghosts of the Land Between the Lakes   by Larry Hillhouse

Ghosts of Lake Norman   by Linda June Furr

To Order Copies

Please send me _____ copies of *Ghosts of the Illinois Canal System* at $9.95 each plus $3.00 S/H. (Make checks payable to Quixote Press.)

Name _____

Street _____

City _____ State _____ Zip _____

QUIXOTE PRESS
3544 Blakslee Street
Wever IA   52658
1-800-571-2665

To Order Copies

Please send me _____ copies of *Ghosts of the Illinois Canal System* at $9.95 each plus $3.00 S/H. (Make checks payable to Quixote Press.)

Name _____

Street _____

City _____ State _____ Zip _____

QUIXOTE PRESS
3544 Blakslee Street
Wever IA   52658
1-800-571-2665